# DAY OF THE DEAD

# DAY OF THE DEAD

## Tony Johnston

### *Illustrated by* Jeanette Winter

**Green Light Readers**
**Clarion Books**
***An Imprint of* HarperCollins *Publishers***
Boston   New York

clarionbooks.com

First Voyager Books edition 2000
*Voyager Books* is a registered trademark of HarperCollins Publishers LLC.
The Library of Congress has cataloged the hardcover edition as follows:
Johnston, Tony, 1942–
Day of the Dead/Tony Johnston; illustrated by Jeanette Winter.
p.  cm.
Summary: Describes a Mexican family preparing
for and celebrating the Day of the Dead.
[1. All Soul's Day—Mexico—Fiction. 2. Mexico—Fiction.]
I. Winter, Jeanette, ill. II. Title.
PZ7.J6478Day 1997
(E)—dc20 96-2276
ISBN 978-0-15-222863-7

ISBN 978-0-15-202446-8 pb

EP  30 29 28 27 26
4500841087

The paintings in this book were done in acrylics on Strathmore Bristol paper.
The display type was set in Serif Gothic Heavy.
The text type was set in Barcelona Medium.
Color separations by Bright Arts, Ltd., Singapore
Printed and bound by Estellaprint, Spain
Production supervision by Ginger Boyer
Designed by Jeanette Winter and Kaelin Chappell

For Jeanette Winter.
And in memory of
Josefina Leal.
—T. J.

In memory of
Signe Maria Ragner.
—J. W.

Above a small town in Mexico,
the sun rises
like a great marigold.

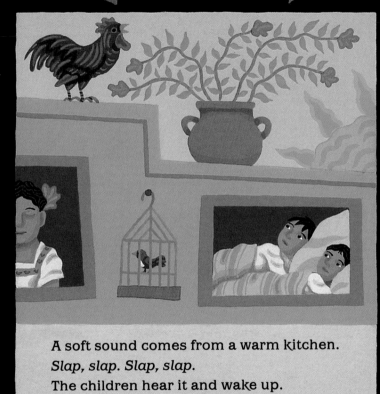

A soft sound comes from a warm kitchen.
*Slap, slap. Slap, slap.*
The children hear it and wake up.

*Mamá* is making *empanadas*,
little pastries fat with meat.

The children crowd around.
*"¡Una probadita! A taste!"*
"Wait," says *mamá. "Espérense."*
"Till when?"
"Soon."

For weeks the family
has been preparing for this day.
*Los tíos*, the uncles, have picked fruit.
Bright oranges, red apples, *tejocotes* of gold.

The children have tried to sneak the fruit.
"Wait," say *los tíos*. *"Espérense."*
"Till when?"
"Soon."

For days *las tías*, the aunts, have been grinding dry *chiles* to powder.

The children have been sniffing the *chile* powder
and sneezing.
"Wait," say *las tías.*
*"HA-CHOO!"* The children sneeze.

PANADERÍA

For days *papá* has been visiting the bakery,
bringing back bulging bundles.

The children have tried to sneak a peek
at what is hidden there.
*Papá* says, "Wait, wait, WAIT."

For days *mamá* has baked *pan de muertos*, bread of the dead.

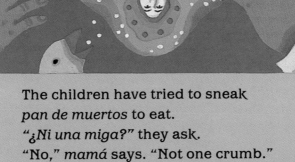

The children have tried to sneak
*pan de muertos* to eat.
"*¿Ni una miga?*" they ask.
"No," *mamá* says. "Not one crumb."

For nights all the family has been making *tamales* for this day.

The children have tried to sneak *tamales* to eat.
*"Espérense."*

Today *papá* has cut up long wands of *caña,* sugarcane.

The children try to sneak the cane pieces
to suck the sweetness out.
"Wait."

Today *las tías* brew a sauce of *chocolate*
and *chile*—a *mole*.
They put chicken in, stirring, stirring again.

The children try to sneak the *mole*—just a taste.
"*Espérense,*" the stirring aunts say.

The children come from the market
with loads of *zempasúchil*, marigolds.

In every room bloom marigold bouquets,
like little glowing suns.

Now night has come.

The family gathers all the things
they have made for this day.
And they go out into the night.

Families from all the houses come carrying
all the things they have made.

Carrying marigolds bright as suns.
And candles like stars.

The little procession goes walking
through the street.
Walking over the hill, walking to
the graveyard where their loved ones lie.

They go dropping a path of petals
for the spirits to find their way.

The family comes to the graves of *los abuelos*, the grandparents.

There they place salt and water in small bowls.
And they place all the things they have made.

They sing.

And they dance.

And they remember *los abuelos*.

"Must we still wait?" ask the children.
"No," says *mamá*. "Eat, eat, EAT."

*Papá* unwraps his bundles.
*¡Calaveras de azúcar!* Sugar skulls!
The children squeal and eat this treat.

*Mamá* slices *pan de muertos.*
Everyone tastes the sweet bread.
One child bites his and—*¡Ay-ay-ay!*—he finds
the tiny, skinny skeleton *mamá* baked inside!

Now it is late.
The family gathers what is left
of all the things they have brought.
They gather platters, jugs, and jars.

They gather their sleeping children.

Upon the graves they leave the marigolds.

Then they go walking, walking home,
carrying candles like stars.

## AUTHOR'S NOTE

The Day of the Dead, *El día de los muertos,*
is one of Mexico's most important holidays.
It actually spans three days, from October 31
to November 2, and is a time to remember
loved ones now gone. Families prepare favorite
foods of the departed and picnic at their
graves. They adorn the graves with marigolds,
the traditional flower of the dead, and strew
paths of petals to lead the spirits to the
offerings, which, along with the delicious food,
usually include salt and water, symbols of
ongoing life. The people dance, sing, and share
memories of their loved ones, welcoming their
spirits, who are thought to return briefly to
take part in the celebration.